KT-873-013

CONTENTS

The Library of Doom is a hidden fortress.
It holds the world's largest collection
of strange and dangerous books.

Behold the Librarian. He defends the Library – and
the world – from super-villains, clever thieves
and fierce monsters. Many of his adventures
have remained secret. Now they can be told.

SECRET #62
BE CAREFUL IN BOOKSHOPS. YOU
NEVER KNOW WHAT YOU'LL FIND.

Chapter One

SECRET STREET

There is a **SECRET** street in every city – if you can find it.

The street is never very long. It is carefully hidden from view.

It is a street **FULL** of bookshops.

The shops look small from the outside. The inside is another matter.

Some are hundreds of metres DEEP. Others have ten or twelve basements.

Each one is full of books and comics and puzzles. And perhaps something else.

A girl called **ROSA** knows about the secret street in her city. She has been there many times.

Today, she holds an umbrella as she **WALKS** down the street.

SH-SH-SH-SH-SH-SH-SH-SH

Rain pours from a dark, grey sky.

The street looks different, Rosa thinks. *It's so empty.*

A strong wind **BLOWS** Rosa's umbrella inside out.

FLOOOOK!

Chapter Two

RATS!

Rosa runs under a WIDE doorway to stay dry. From there, she sees her favourite bookshop down the street.

The store is called Hungry for Books.

A sign hangs above the door. It shows a **LARGE** mouth with lips that are painted gold.

Mr Hammer is the owner. He
loves books, but he does not like pets.

A sign in his window says:
NO PETS ALLOWED!

Then Rosa spots small shadows moving across the street. They **RUSH** inside Mr Hammer's store.

Rats! thinks Rosa.

The girl pulls her umbrella back into shape. She runs to Mr Hammer's shop.

Her shoes **SPLASH** through cold rain puddles.

Overhead, the bookshop's sign **SWINGS** in the wind.

For a second, Rosa thinks she sees sharp teeth in the painted mouth.

But they are just raindrops **DRIPPING** from the golden lips.

CH-CH-CH-CH-CH-CH-CH-CH

Rosa yelps as three rats **SCURRY** over her wet shoes.

Rosa follows the rats inside Hungry for Books. She shuts the door behind her.

CH-CH-CH-CH-CH-CH-CH-CH

Outside, more rats **SCRATCH** at the shop's door.

Rosa hears the rats' tiny claws scraping against the wood.

The girl SHIVERS and turns away.

She steps further into the shop and looks around.

"Mr Hammer!" **SHOUTS** Rosa. "Hello?"

There is <u>no</u> answer.

Chapter Three

THE BASEMENT DOOR

Rosa **WALKS** to the shop's front desk. Whenever she visits, Mr Hammer is always sitting there.

Today, the chair is empty.

The shop is **COLD** and full of shadows.

Then Rosa hears a **VOICE**.

"Help me-e-e-e-e!"

It sounds like Mr Hammer.

"Where are you?" Rosa calls out.

KREEE-EE-EEEKKK!

Rosa sees the shop's basement door open by itself.

Small shadows run down the stairs.
The door opens WIDER.

"Help me-e-e-e!"

Mr Hammer's voice is coming from the basement.

"I'll go and get help!" calls Rosa. She **TURNS** to leave.

Then she hears the rats clawing at the door. She remembers the creatures **RUNNING** over her shoes.

Rosa **CAN'T** go outside.

Instead, she turns back and walks towards the basement stairs.

A dim light GLOWS at the bottom.

Slowly, Rosa's feet lead her down the steps.

Chapter Four

HUNGRY FOR BOOKS

At the bottom of the steps, the glow is brighter.

Rosa sees a **LARGE** room. The walls are lined with bookshelves.

In the middle of the room is a large, shadowy shape.

As Rosa walks closer, she sees it is not a single shape. It is a circle of creatures in **HAIRY** coats.

One of the creatures turns to look at Rosa.

It is a huge rat in human clothing. The rat is nibbling on a book.

"No, no! You can't!" **SHOUTS** a man.

Mr Hammer is surrounded by the huge rats. He holds a pile of **OLD** books to his chest.

The creatures **SCRATCH** at the covers.

"No, I won't let you eat these!" yells Mr Hammer.

More big rats turn to stare at Rosa.

"You look as tasty as a book," one of them SQUEAKS.

Then Rosa hears a whisper in her ear.

"Hold out your umbrella," it tells her.

Rosa points her open umbrella at the creatures. The rats hiss **ANGRILY**.

Rosa wants to **RUN** away, but she can't leave Mr Hammer.

The voice whispers to her again. *"What kinds of books do you find at this shop?"* it asks.

The giant rats start **CRAWLING** towards Rosa.

Chapter Five

CATALOGUE

"Hurry," says the voice. *"Name the different types of books."*

Rosa whispers, "Fiction books and non-fiction books."

The umbrella begins **TWIRLING** in her hands.

"Ghost stories and funny stories," she says more LOUDLY.

The umbrella twirls faster.

Rosa's voice GROWS stronger. "Books about animals, dinosaurs and sport," she says.

The umbrella whirls her VOICE throughout the basement.

Rosa's voice RINGS in the creatures' large ears.

They cover their ears with hairy claws. They **GROWL** and snap their jaws.

But Rosa doesn't stop.

"Fantasy books, history books, joke books!" she **SHOUTS**.

The rats can't stand the noise.

Suddenly, they **RUSH** past Rosa and scamper up the stairs.

Mr Hammer is lying on the basement floor.

He is still holding his most **VALUABLE** books.

Rosa's umbrella stops **TWIRLING**.

Mr Hammer looks **UP** at Rosa. "Thank you," he says.

"But I don't understand," Rosa says. "Who was whispering in my ear?"

"Didn't you see that man talking to you?" asks Mr Hammer. "He's right behind you."

Rosa turns. A **STRANGE** man is standing in the shadows.

He is the LIBRARIAN.

"You were naming *cat*egories of books," says the Librarian. "And those rats **HATE** anything with the word *CAT*."

Rosa smiles at the hero.

Mr Hammer **STANDS** up.

"Well, that does it," says the bookshop owner as they all start walking up the stairs. "Tomorrow I'm putting a new sign in my window."

"ALL CATS ARE WELCOME!"

GLOSSARY

catalogue a list of things, such as books or names, ordered in a particular way

category a group of things that are alike

creature a living thing, often one that is unusual or strange

dim not bright

nibble to eat with small bites

scamper to run or move around quickly

surround to be on all sides of someone or something

twirl to spin something around and around

valuable worth a lot of money

TALK ABOUT IT

1. How do you think Rosa felt as she walked into Hungry for Books? How would you have felt? Would you have gone into the basement?

2. Why do you think the rat creatures were in the bookshop? Point to examples in the story to back up your answer.

WRITE ABOUT IT

1. Rosa lists categories of books to scare away the rats. What kind of book is your favourite? Write two paragraphs explaining your choice.

2. The secret street has many bookshops. What other things might be hiding away in them? Write a story about a new bookshop and a new danger. Make sure you make it exciting!

ABOUT THE AUTHOR

Michael Dahl is an award-winning author of more than 200 books for young people. He especially likes to write scary or weird fiction. His latest series are the sci-fi adventure Escape from Planet Alcatraz and School Bus of Horrors. As a child, Michael spent lots of time in libraries. "The creepier, the better," he says. These days, besides writing, he likes travelling and hunting for the one, true door that leads to the Library of Doom.

ABOUT THE ILLUSTRATOR

Patricio Clarey was born in Argentina. He graduated in fine arts from the Martín A. Malharro School of Visual Arts, specializing in illustration and graphic design. Patricio currently lives in Barcelona, Spain, where he works as a freelance graphic designer and illustrator. He has created several comics and graphic novels, and his work has been featured in books and other publications.